First published in 1995 by Viking,
a division of Penguin Books USA Inc.

10 9 8 7 6 5 4 3 2

Printed in Singapore. Set in Bembo.

Library of Congress
Cataloging-in-Publication Data

Kalman, Maira.
    Swami on rye : Max in India / Maira Kalman.
      p. cm.
  Summary: Max, the famous dog-poet and
Hollywood director, faces fatherhood and searches for
the meaning of life in exotic India.
    ISBN 0-670-85646-0
    [1. Dogs–Fiction. 2. India–Fiction.] I. Title.
PZ7.K1256Sw 1995
[Fic]–dc20   95-9749
                                                  CIP
                                                  AC

Swami on Rye

Max in India

Maira Kalman

Viking

Published by the Penguin Group
Penguin Books USA Inc.
375 Hudson Street New York, New York 10014 USA
Penguin Books Ltd, 27 Wrights Lane, London W8 5TZ, England
Penguin Books Australia Ltd, Ringwood, Victoria, Australia
Penguin Books Canada Ltd, 10 Alcorn Ave., Toronto, Ontario, Canada M4V 3B2
Penguin Books (N.Z.) Ltd. 182-190 Wairau Road, Auckland 10, New Zealand

Penguin Books Ltd, Registered Offices: Harmondsworth, Middlesex, England

I had to have a herring in a hurry.

One minute you're sitting
quietly in your room, when the
doorbell rings. You knock over

This is life.

a glass of water, run to open the
door, and someone **throws** a wet
sock on your head.

And so it was that Crêpes, my wife,
was composing an opera. (Arias. Divas. Credenzas.)
And at the same time, like a glowing golden kernel,
she was growing.

She was pregnant.

I was elated.
I was deflated.
I was delirious with joy.
I was itchy.
I was ticklish.
I was all things confused. Life was so big. And I was so small.

Yet I had really important
things to do.
Like get Crêpes the stinky
herring snacks that she craved.
So I was dispatched
(Mr. Second Fiddle,
Mr. Don't-Get-in-the-Way)
to Hairy Harry's Fish Shop.

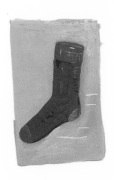

I left the house muttering,
WHODOESSHETHINKSHEIS?
WHATISTHEMEANINGOFITTOTHINKTHAT?
WHATIFIDIDATHINGORTWO?
WHATAMIADOG?
and other assorted unmutterables.

Bumping along
on the subway
my mind
is bouncing
from fish
to knish
to gibberish
when

this guy
(red jacket)
bops
(black shoes)
into
the train car

and starts
to play
this licorice stick.

And I get this funny feeling
in my stomach
that something

big

is going to happen when a woman
(orange plaid suit, chair on head)
hands me a piece of paper,
raises her eyebrows three times,
and walks away.

This was **preposterous.**

This was **mysterious.**

This was **ridiculous.**

But when the ridiculous knocks,

            I answer.

MAX!

Get off at the next stop.
Walk past Mr. Biddi Beedi's
Snake Charming School
to the Magic Lantern
Restaurant.
You will not be sorry.

Sincerely,
Karisma Kapoor

The light inside
the Magic Lantern
was blue and dim.
A willowy woman wafted toward me.

"Welcome Max.
Refresh yourself with
this nectar of
hummingbird hums,
fire of fireflies,
and cheese juice."
I sipped the shot,
which hit the spot.
Then I saw a man sitting
in the corner.
Nothing unusual
there.

But then (aha!)
my (b)eagle eye noticed
he was hovering
three feet off the ground.

"Ah Max, at long last we meet. I am Vivek Shabaza-zaza-za. That's za-zaza-za. Not za-za-za-za or za-za za za, please."

He placed his palms together, touched his fingertips to his forehead and said,

"*Namaste.* [Canasta?]
I am your genial genie,
　　　your garrulous guru,
　　　your suave swami.
When we are alive
　　　(which we are),
　　we are bound to ask
ourselves, as we become parents,
or get a horriblestuffyrednose,
　　or worse yet
　　　lose our favorite
　　lucky button, 'What (after all)
　is the Meaning (anyway) of Life?
Why? Why? Why are we here?
Where did we come from? Where are we going?'
The answer, dear Max, is at the end of a twisty and turny
road (full of slippery banana peels),
and I am tickled to take you on
this **pickle** of a journey."

And not giving me a second to protest (or to spell MISSISSIPPI)
he sneezed three times, and a small carpet (magic? puce?)
lifted us up into the sky. Being extremely brave,
I shut my eyes and **SHRIEKED FOR 47 SECONDS.**

Then I heard Vivek say, "Max, be bold! Max, behold!"

I opened my eyes. Dizzy. Dumbstruck. Dazzled. We were flying over an
there was so much happening happening. I gaped.

This is what I saw:
2 golden temples
1 giant **shoe.**

Shacks made
from **tin**, sticks,
cardboard,
and cloth.

Women in
flowing saris
of turquoise,
shimmering
pink, saffron,
and tangerine.

Vendors selling tires,
teapots, jasmine, candy,
coriander, **beetles**, bat
wings, thermometers,
back scratchers,
fake noses,
beds, pianos, and
itching powder.

I saw clattering
carts, careening
buses, rickshaws,
honking taxis,
ragpickers,
ear cleaners,
soothsayers and
forsoothsayers.

exotic and teeming metropolis. I couldn't figure out what was happening, I gawked. I oggled. I saw the impossible possibled.

I saw six people riding on a bicycle.

A man with **triangles** around his head.

And a man carrying six **chairs** on his head.

A woman carrying four baskets of **fish** on her head and four fish carrying a basket of women on their heads.

And oblivious to the din, ruckus, heat, flies, frantic tumult, and general madness, COWS were nonchalantly strolling down the street.

"Holy cow," I murmured.

"Absolutely," said Vivek.

"Vivek, where are we?"

"In India Max.

Listen: You can't get a sour pickle in New Delhi,

and we call TV the 'telly.'

A swami won't eat salami,

he can live on water and air.

He can't get enough of that minimalist fare.

A Brahman would blanch if you offered him meat.

For upper-caste guys, lentil's a treat.

Or curry or chutney or a dollop of dal.

We might eat with our hands,

as we sit on the floor.

Your staid Western customs

just throw out the door.

You're in India now,

in in India now.

We've been here forever

despite the hot weather.

In Calcutta the people are packed like sardines.

In Madras they run.

In Bombay they're bombastic.

In Bengal they hunted the tiger fantastic.

In Simla it's cool

in the hills by the pool,

as the British decided as a rule in their rule.

You're in India now,

in in India now.

Don a new turban.

Stand on your head.

You'll get new perspective

on the lives that you've led."

"Holy Hindustan," I croaked.

"What does that mean?"

"It means that you are an old soul
and that life is a wheel," Vivek murmured.

"I'm wearing old shoes and life's a banana peel?"

"We live many
lives, Max.
And each life
brings us
closer to
the truth."

"What truth?"

"The truth
that resides
in the
third eye."

"Is that
anything like
having two
left feet?"

"As the bulbul bird barks you shall see."
I was just trying to imagine a barking
bird, when a tremendous noise
overwhelmed us.

A brigade of **red** motorcycles roared around the corner pulling a gargantuan statue of the Great God Ganesh surrounded by dozens of gyrating dancers and saxophone-playing snakes.

"Holy Madras!" I yelped. "What was that?"

"Make-believe. Fantasy. Suspension of reality," announced Vivek gleefully.

"Cast of thousands. Singing. Dancing. Can you guess? Of course you can: It's a movie. I adore movies, don't you? When that wooden boy with the long nose rescues his father from the whale, I weep like a baby. When the sea parts, I think, 'Now that is a miracle.' I love every delicious second. You have to be a real *falooda* not to love a movie."

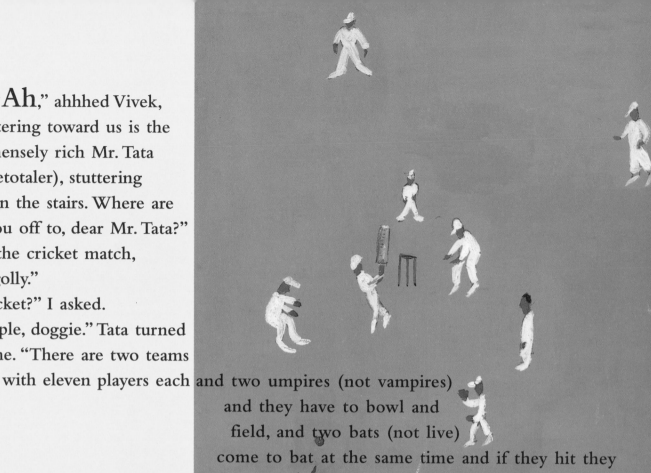

"Ah," ahhhed Vivek, "Tottering toward us is the immensely rich Mr. Tata (a teetotaler), stuttering down the stairs. Where are you off to, dear Mr. Tata?"

"To the cricket match, by golly."

"Cricket?" I asked.

"Simple, doggie." Tata turned to me. "There are two teams with eleven players each and two umpires (not vampires) and they have to bowl and field, and two bats (not live) come to bat at the same time and if they hit they can score six runs and if a batsman hits in the air and any fielder goes up and catches it directly, it's out. But if the ball is bowled and the batsman misses and the bowler hits the stump, he's bowled (and if he hits the player on the head that is not cricket), but if one has to go to run and does not do the run and if they hit the wickets he is stumped. And that would be a sticky wicket and the game would last three or four days and that is that.

"Ta-ta," said Tata.

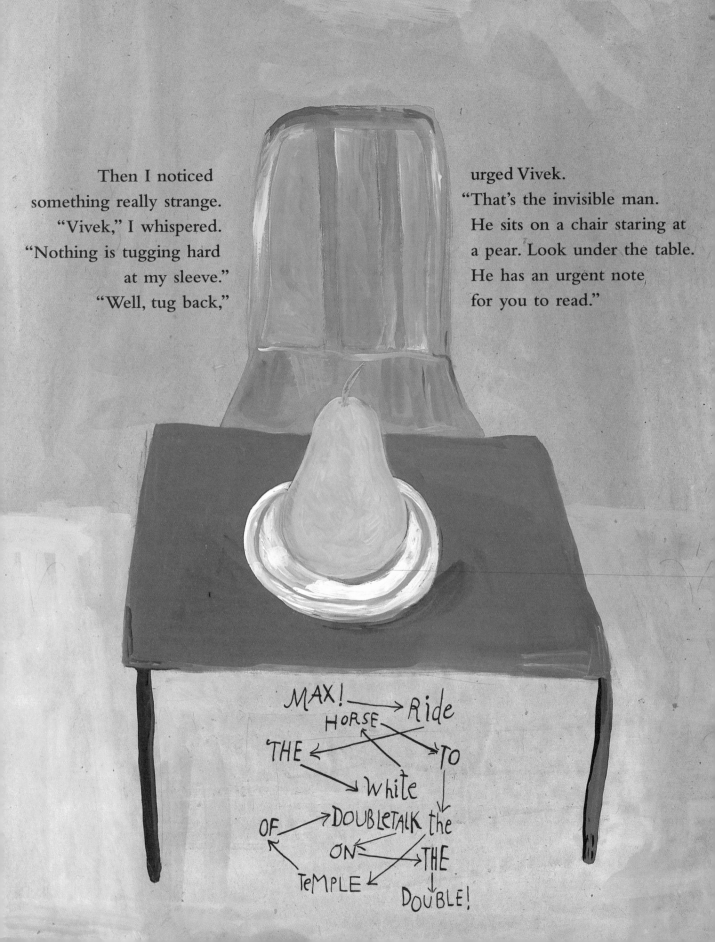

Then I noticed
something really strange.
"Vivek," I whispered.
"Nothing is tugging hard
at my sleeve."
"Well, tug back,"

urged Vivek.
"That's the invisible man.
He sits on a chair staring at
a pear. Look under the table.
He has an urgent note
for you to read."

Ride I did,
right into the inner chamber of the
outer belly button
of the sacred temple.

Sitting on a mountain of lentils was a charming two-headed chap.

He
(THEY)
started talking
very, very
fast

What is the meaning
WHAT IS THE MEANING
of life
OF WAKING ME UP
and what is the meaning
AND ONLY GIVING ME
of egg on my face
ONE FRIED EGG
and if everything is nothing
WHEN I LIKE POACHED
and nothing is everything
WITH TOAST ON THE SIDE
then not for nothing
THUS I KNOW
do I say
THAT THE SALUKA
nothing from nothing
WHO MADE THE EGG
equals something.
IS REALLY GOOD FOR NOTHING.

"What was
he they
talking talking
about about?"

Meanwhile...

in the midst of rehearsal
in a cool Carnegie Hall studio
(rent controlled),
paws poised, baton midair,
Crêpes felt a flutter,
then a devilish dervish, and she knew
that the rehearsal would have to be postponed.

The inevitable was unavoidable.

She was about to have the babies. SOON!

Crêpes phoned Max.
No answer.

She called Ida,

    who called Bruno,

        who accidentally called his dry cleaner,
the meticulous Mr. Prokofiev.

But Max was nowhere to be found.
    Where could that soon-to-be-dad be?

A pathway of gardens
and fountains
led up to the
gleaming white palace.
There once lived a ruler
named Shah Jehan.
His riches were vast, but his
greatest treasure by far was
his beloved wife,
Mumtaz Mahal.

When she died,
heartbroken and alone
he built a monument
to her memory.
The Taj Mahal.
They say it took 20,000 workers
21 years to build the Taj,
or 21 workers 20,000 years,
Vivek wasn't sure which.

What epic love!
What divine devotion!
He really liked her a lot.

I thought of my life with Crêpes,
and though I could not shower
her with jewels, I could shower
her with words
of love.

For you my luscious fig,
  the Taj Mahal wouldn't be too big.
    For you my sweet paratha,
      I'd write a poem l o n g e r than the Mahabharata.
      I'd walk backwards over the Himalayas,
        if you'd spend with me your nights and dayas.
        For the maharani I adore,
          I'd steal the priceless Kohinoor.
        I'd meditate,
  I'd levitate,
to hear you say,
"That dog is great."
  For you my learned guru,
    I'd learn to speak Urdu.
      And for my true-blue fakir,
        I'd pluck the rarest rose from Kashmir.
        I'd practice ahimsa
        for just one quick glimpsa
      your pure clear white soul,
    the one that knows all.
So come my darling Darjeeling,
my prize, my JEWEL,
  my everything.
      Our karma can't be clearer.
      There's no one I hold dearer.
        No fata morgana,
      it's you that I wanna
share nirvana with.

And with my face turned up toward the
heavens (drop), my eyes closed in
rapture (drop), I felt (drop) a drop.
One hundred black umbrellas opened, pop . . . pop . . . pop,
as the fat raindrops began to

drop

drop

drop.

"Monsoon,"
said Vivek.
"Three
months of
rain,
rain,
rain, and
then it's
really hot
again."

Drowning in longing for the one I loved, I cried out,
"I wish to go home; could you kindly
snap it up with the meaning of life?"
"Let's go to the mountain," Vivek counseled.
"And as the fish flies you shall find the answer there."

We continued our journey.

We passed a boy with dots
playing a drum.

We passed women dancing.

We passed a man

walking up a blue ladder onto the back of an elephant.

"I can't help but notice, Vivek,"
I said, as we stopped at a blue-leafed
tree, "that this is a most
unusual and
wondrous country."

"Max, you speak the truth,"
said Vivek. "Listen:

"Under a budding bodhi tree
sat a pudgy unbudging buddha.
For 49 days not a worda
no eating, no drinking
just thinking unblinking
could you do the same?
I'm not surah."

Vivek picked up a **black rock**
with **two eyes** painted on it.
Suddenly he began to shimmer. He began to glow.
And in front of my dumbstruck nose he turned into a panther,

then into
the great ballerina
Anna Pavlova and
her
husband Victor Dandré.

Then

A GLASS
OF WATER,

A PORCUPINE
NAMED PINKY,

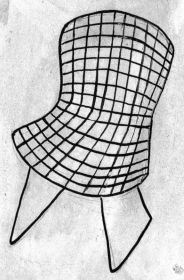

A PAIR OF
PLAID PANTS,

A HAT OR JELL-O MOLD
(I COULDN'T TELL WHICH),

A RED SPORTS CAR,

MY AUNT BESSIE
(THE WEIGHT LIFTER),

AN ICE POP,

DANNY KAYE,

A CHAIR I'VE BEEN WANTING,

and **finally** into
a little old man
with a brown hat and
very thick glasses.
"By golly. By Gandhi. And holy-moly," I squealed. "Is that you, Vivek?"

FIRST YOU MUST PEEL A LEMON AND PUT THE PEEL*Lavander Honey*

ED SLICES INTO A TEAPOT. THEN TAKE THE BOILING WATER FROM THE STOVE

HONEY. STIR IT UP. PUT ON PAJAMAS. GET INTO BED. POUR TODDY INTO MUG. SIP.

AND POUR IT INTO THE TEAPOT. POUR IN SOME

"Yes, Max. I will now
reveal to you the Meaning
of Life. Please take this
package and deliver it
to Crêpes.

"Now Max, the secret of life is
HA...HA...HA...HA..."

Why was he laughing?
"HA...HA...HA..."

What was happening?
"...HA-CHOOO!!!"

"I am afraid, Max, that I have
caught a cold and must get
right into bed with a nice
hot toddy.
    No time for the meaning
of life, but don't worry,
    my friend,
        you will figure it out.

"In three snips you will be back where you belong.
Keep in touch.   Lovely meeting you.
Fabulous fun.
All the best."

And with that, he vanished.

The corridor was shining.
And people were rushing around
in green smocks and masks.
Morris and Ida were running toward me
wild-eyed, pulling me by my sleeve.
Frantic. Urgent.

"Max! Where on earth have you been?"

"You'll never believe this, but I went to India."

"No time for your jokes, Max. It's TIME!!!"

And suddenly,
I realized
where I was:

I made a dash for the room.
I tripped.
I knocked over
a glass of water.

The brown package flew through the air, unwrapping, revealing a herring, which sailed through the window.

I ran across the slippery
white floor, past the window
with the curtain

blowing in the breeze,

past a chair that I'm pretty sure was green,

and into the arms of Crêpes.

(Ha-chooo!)
"Bless you Max."
"I didn't sneeze."
"Well then who did?"

And all was revealed to me
as we became
a family of three . . .

No, four . . .

"Harriet, did you see that fish
flying out the window?"
"Harry, you are always seeing fish.
You have to change jobs."

"Mr. Know-It-All, Mr. High-and-Mighty."
Who do you think you are, Nizam Hyderabad?"
"If you lived a thousand lives you would still be a worm."
"For one million rupees I would not exchange turbans with you."
"May onions grow out of your bellybutton."
"May you quack like a duck."

No, five.

Whatalife!

There's nothing nicer
than a nice hot toddy and
a good book
in bed.

Enda.